This **ELMER** book belongs to:

. . . .

For Roberta Hazel

This paperback edition first published in 2021 by Andersen Press Ltd.
First published in Great Britain in 2020 by Andersen Press Ltd.,
20 Vauxhall Bridge Road, London SW1V 2SA.
Copyright © David McKee, 2020.
The right of David McKee to be identified as the author and
illustrator of this work has been asserted by him in accordance
with the Copyright, Designs and Patents Act, 1988.
All rights reserved.
Colour separated in Switzerland by Photolitho AG, Zürich.
Printed and bound in China.
1   3   5   7   9   10   8   6   4   2
British Library Cataloguing in Publication Data available.
ISBN 978 1 78344 949 1

ELMER
and the
LOST TREASURE

David McKee

Andersen Press

Elmer, the patchwork elephant, was with his cousin Wilbur and three other elephants.
"Good morning," called Tiger. "Where are you going so bright and early?"
"On a long, exploring walk," said Elmer.
"Well, I'm having a long, exploring dream," said Lion.

After they'd been walking for
quite some time, the explorers found
themselves in a part of the jungle that
none of them knew. The undergrowth
became darker and thicker. They took it
in turns to push their way through.

Elmer was leading when, with a loud, "Oooh!" he disappeared.
The others stopped and stared.
"Elmer!" they called. "Are you all right?"

Elmer's voice came back. "I'm fine. Come on down.
Be careful – it's a steep slope."

So, slipping and sliding,
    rocking and rolling,
        oohing and aaahing,
            giggling and gasping,
                the others joined Elmer.

Once they'd recovered, Elmer said,
"Now, come and see this."
He led them through a curtain of plants.
"Look," he said, and there was the
entrance to a kind of palace.
"WOW!" said the elephants.

"What are we waiting for?" said Wilbur. "Let's take a look." He and Elmer went through the door.

An elephant held the others back and said, "The famous Lost Treasure of the jungle must be hidden here. Don't tell Elmer – we'll find it and surprise him."

Elmer and Wilbur were admiring a large hall when
the others scuttled past in the side corridors.

"What are they playing at?" said Elmer.
"Probably hide-and-seek," said Wilbur.

A little later Elmer and Wilbur were surprised to see
the elephants standing one on the other. The top
one was searching the head of a wooden sculpture.
"We thought we saw something," one explained.
"Fascinating," said Elmer.

Soon after that, the cousins were admiring some
mosaics and wall paintings when the others sneaked
past on tip-toe.
"Stranger and stranger," said Elmer.
"And stranger," added Wilbur.

The next time the other elephants were seen they were standing in a dry fountain.

"What are you looking for?" Elmer asked.

"Oh!" said the elephants in surprise. "Oh! We were ah... wondering if the fountain still worked."

"There's a lever here," said Elmer, as he pulled it.
"Shower time."
Wilbur chuckled. "I think we should be heading
home," he said.
"You're right," said Elmer.
"Time to go!" they called to the others.

On the way home an elephant said, "That was a fun day. Pity we didn't find the Lost Treasure." Elmer and Wilbur stared. "We thought you knew – the whole place was the Lost Treasure."

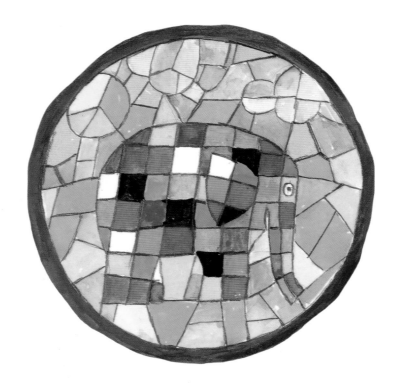